AMULET BOOKS • NEW YORK

MARYA KHAN

❀ AND THE ❀
INCREDIBLE HENNA PARTY

written by
SAADIA FARUQI

illustrated by
ANI BUSHRY

Cataloging-in-Publication Data has been applied for and may be obtained from the Library of Congress.

ISBN 978-1-4197-6116-4

Text © 2022 Saadia Faruqi
Illustrations © 2022 Ani Bushry
Cover design by Deena Fleming
Book design by Kay Petronio

Printed and bound in U.S.A.
10 9 8 7 6 5 4 3 2 1

Amulet Books are available at special discounts when purchased in quantity for premiums and promotions as well as fundraising or educational use. Special editions can also be created to specification. For details, contact specialsales@abramsbooks.com or the address below.

ABRAMS The Art of Books
195 Broadway, New York, NY 10007
abramsbooks.com

FOR MY SISTERS
AND ALL THE
TIMES WE GOT
HENNA AT THE
BEAUTY PARLOR
THE NIGHT
BEFORE EID

WORD OF THE DAY

ELEPHANT

A very large

mammal with a

trunk and tusks

I t wasn't fair that my birthday was exactly two days after Alexa R.'s. "Why couldn't I have been born a little early?" I groaned at breakfast on Monday.

"This again?" Mama frowned at me over her teacup. "Why do you say the same thing every year, Marya?"

"Because my birthday is after hers every year," I pointed out. How could she forget? She's my mother. "Alexa is the most annoying person on the planet."

Mama sighed and went back to her tea. "No, she isn't. She's our next-door neighbor."

Actually, Alexa was more than just our neighbor. She was also in my third-grade class, where she sat at the same table as me and my best friend, Hanna. Every single day. Being annoying. And two days older.

"Two days is nothing," my sister Aliyah said, waving her paratha around. "Wait till you get to my age. Then you won't even care."

I rolled my eyes. Aliyah was now officially

a teenager, so she acted all smart and mature. Which she wasn't, of course. There were smears of egg yolk on her cheek and her paratha was falling all over the table. I giggled and she gave me a glare with her laser eyes.

"*Anyway*," I said, turning to Mama. "Alexa always has a huge party, and then I have . . . nothing. How is that justice?"

"Justice?" Mama smiled at me. "I see you're making good use of that Word of the Day diary I bought you."

I shook my finger at her. "Don't try to change the subject."

"Then stop comparing yourself to your friends, please. It's never a good idea." Mama put down her cup. "Now hurry up and eat. I have to get to the shop after I drop you kids off at school."

I groaned again. Mama owned a flower shop downtown, and her van was, like, a hundred years old. Whenever she dropped us at school, I always ended up with potting soil stains on my clothes.

"Your van is always full of plants and things. Can't Baba take us?"

Mama gave me a look. "He already left for work. He had to be there early today."

"Plants are a good thing," Aliyah told me like I was two years old. Then she patted my head with her greasy paratha-hand.

I jumped up from my chair. "Ugh, stop! Mama, tell her to stop!"

"Stop, Aliyah," Mama said calmly. "And wash your hands please."

"You're such a baby," Aliyah hissed at me.

I grabbed my backpack from the floor and rushed out of the kitchen before she gave me the evil eye or something. Not that I believed in that sort of thing, but our dadi definitely did. She was Baba's mom, and she lived with us. She's told me hundreds of stories about jinn and the evil eye and witches with long hair and backward feet. They're the best stories ever, all warm and creepy.

Only you should never, ever listen to them at

bedtime. Or you'll have the most awful dreams. I'm not kidding.

"Fifteen minutes!" Mama called from the kitchen. "And tell your brother to wake up!"

"Why is it always my job to wake Sal up?" I whined, but I was pretty sure nobody heard me. I banged on Sal's door and screamed "WAKE UP!"

"Go away!" he screamed back. "I'm already up."

Yeah, right.

"Who's that?" came Dadi's stern voice from her bedroom. I peeked in. She was watching one of her Pakistani dramas on YouTube, hooked up to a small TV on the dresser.

"Sorry, I was trying to wake Sal up."

"Who's this Sal?" she grumbled. "Say his full name, Salman."

"Sorry," I said again, coming into her room and flopping on the bed. Dadi's room was always dark (because she kept the curtains on her window tightly closed) and always smelled of Vicks. It was my comfort place. My hideout.

Dadi looked at me from behind her thick

glasses. "What's wrong, birthday girl?" she asked.

"It's not today, Dadi!" I told her. "It's next week. Remember?"

"You're still the birthday girl." Dadi went back to her show. "Look, it's her birthday too."

I turned my head to stare at the screen. A teenage girl was dressed up in a bright red shalwar kameez, with flowers in her hair and henna on her hands. There was a band playing music, a table full of food, and hundreds of people. "I

thought that was a wedding or something," I gasped, my eyes round like plates.

Dadi shook her head. "She's a very rich girl."

I sighed and slumped back on the bed. "Like Alexa."

"Who?"

"You know, our next-door neighbor. The giant house with the pool and everything?"

Dadi shrugged. "Does she have an elephant?"

"What?" I quickly looked at the TV again. There was an elephant at the party now, giving rides to kids like they were at a zoo.

Unbelievable.

"Why can't we be like that?" I cried, waving my arm around.

Dadi shook her head. "That's just a story, Marya jaan, not real life. Besides, where would you even keep an elephant?"

I suddenly thought of my tiny closet, with a giant gray elephant stuck inside. I grinned.

Dadi also grinned. "See, it's funny."

We watched the show together. It was in Urdu, but I understood what was going on. Mostly. Okay, only a little bit. But the party with the fancy dresses and music and dancing was fun to watch.

A few minutes later, I heard Mama call again. "Marya! Where are you?"

Yikes! I had to get to school before first bell or I'd have another tardy. Mama said I collect them like seashells at the beach. I scrambled up from the bed. "Tell me what happens later," I told Dadi.

"Be good. Study hard. Get all A's," she replied without even looking up. Like she did every single day.

Yeah right. That was Alexa, not me. "I'll try," I replied.

2

WORD OF THE DAY

RADIOACTIVE

Giving out

a dangerous

energy

mama's van didn't start right away. She had to turn the key six times. She had that scrunched-up look on her face that meant she's NOT HAPPY WITH THINGS. Then the van gave a splutter and started.

I clapped, and Sal rolled his eyes at me. I rolled my eyes right back at him. Just because he was in fifth grade, he thought he was something else.

"Thank God!" Mama muttered. She was wearing a pink flowery hijab, the one I really liked.

"Ugh, why does this always happen?" Aliyah hissed from the front seat. She was always hissing, like she'd forgotten how to speak like a normal person. Or maybe she was a big fan of snakes or something. Who knew what went on in her witchy head?

Mama just ignored her and reversed out of the driveway really fast. There was a pile of bags on the backseat where I was sitting. They kept leaning into me as Mama drove down the streets toward school. I tried pushing them away with

both hands, but the smell was too funky for pot-ting soil.

"Ew, what is that?" Aliyah cried, looking back at me.

"It's just supplies for my shop," Mama told her. "I have a big event this weekend."

Mama's shop was always full of flowers. Lots and lots of flowers. Plus, plants and bushes and tiny Japanese trees called bonsai. Whenever someone in our town had a wedding, they asked Mama to supply the flowers.

The van turned a corner and the pile of bags pushed into me again. I pushed back.

Then I saw the label on the bags. *Fertilizer.*

"Do you even know what fertilizer is made of?" I grumbled. "Radioactive poop, that's what." Well, maybe not the radioactive part. But it's still poop and other gross things.

"Stop exaggerating," Mama replied.

"Don't let that fall on your clothes, Marya," Sal told me slyly. "You'll attract all the insects from the schoolyard."

"No, I won't!" I said, but I stopped touching the pile very quickly. Sal started talking about fertilizer and how it was made. Disgusting.

I turned to the front. "So, Mama, about my birthday—"

Mama shushed me with a finger. "No more talk of this. You'll invite Hanna for pizza and cake on Sunday, and that's it. Like always."

I turned back with a sigh. *Always* sucked big-time.

My best friend, Hanna, was waiting for me at our regular spot in school: the big glass case with all the sports trophies. Whoever got there first (it was never me) waited for the other person there. We'd chosen it because Hanna loved sports, especially soccer. Her dad used to be a soccer player in Egypt.

"What's that smell?" Hanna asked, sniffing. Her long braid swished as she moved her head around. What was she, a detective?

I sniffed too. "I don't smell anything," I muttered. Okay, I know I'm not supposed to lie, but this was an emergency. I couldn't really admit to sitting next to a bag of poop, could I?

RRRING! The bell rang and saved me. Phew!

Our third-grade classroom was next to the school playground, which was a good thing, because I could stare out the windows at the swings. I didn't do it all the time, though. Just when everything got to be too much.

Like right now. Alexa R. flopped down in the seat in front of me with a smile like she was the Queen of England. Her blond hair was so straight and shiny it looked like a silky curtain. And her dress was a pretty pink color with black dots. Who even wears fancy dresses to school?

I tried to look out the window, but it didn't really help, because our desks faced each other in little squares of four students each. The whole class was set up like that, squares made up of four desks. Our square was me, Hanna, Alexa, and an empty seat where Tobias used to sit until he moved to Dallas.

I hated the squares. They meant I had to stare at Alexa and her Queen of England smile all day. Every day.

"Hello, Marya. It's my birthday this week, you know," Alexa whispered.

I pretended I didn't hear her. It was my birthday too, but did you see me bragging about it?

"I have invitations for the whole class," she continued, patting her backpack. Her glittery unicorn backpack that her dad had gotten her from Paris. I knew this because she'd told the entire class on the first day of school.

I couldn't care less if I never went to Paris. I bet it was boring.

To stop myself from thinking about Paris, I looked out at the playground. The swings were big and blue, with long twisty chains made of shiny metal. I wished I could sit on them right now. I tried to calculate how many minutes to recess. I liked doing math in my head. It made me forget about annoying people and their annoying birthday talk.

Thankfully, our teacher, Miss Piccolo, didn't like talking in class either. She slapped her desk really hard and started the first lesson. It was social studies—not my favorite. Miss Piccolo passed out worksheets and said, "Work together in your desk groups, please!" Ugh. That wasn't my favorite either.

I took my worksheet and put it right in front of my face like I couldn't read it properly.

"What are you doing?" Hanna whispered. "It's just a big map."

I pulled the worksheet away from me. Hanna was right. There was a blank map of the United

States, and then lots of questions under it, like *What is the largest state?* and *What is the smallest state?* And we had to color the map, like babies.

Alexa waved her arm to show her fancy brace-lets. "I can do this all by myself," she boasted. "I've been to twenty-seven states, you know."

Suddenly, I figured out why Aliyah hissed like a snake when she was mad. I narrowed my eyes and leaned forward until my nose almost touched Alexa's. "I can too, you—"

I stopped, because she was making a horrible face right at me. "Ew!" she yelled really loudly. "You smell like poop, Marya Khan!"

3

WORD OF THE DAY

INVITATION

A request to

go somewhere or

do something

t recess, I ran to the swings like I was being chased by a bear. A bear wearing a pink dress and holding a bunch of papers in her hand.

I knew what those papers were: her birthday invitations.

Guess who didn't have any invitations to hand out? Me, that's who. I never got a big party.

"Gather round!" Alexa shouted, just like Principal Cleveland when he had something important to say.

The kids in my class all flocked to Alexa like she was a celebrity.

Not me. I jumped onto a swing and started to push myself up and down. Maybe if I went really fast, the smell of poop would be carried away by the wind. Maybe I could pretend I wasn't at Harold Smithers Elementary School's tiny playground at all.

Where else could I be? Not Paris, because that was boring. New York City? Oh, that sounded like fun. Or Karachi, where Mama and Baba were born. I'd visited Karachi only once, when I was a baby. Aliyah remembered it, but Sal and I didn't.

Alexa looked over at me. "Are you coming, Marya?" she called out.

I ignored her. That didn't help, though. She stomped over to the swings like she was on a mission. Hanna and the other kids from our class followed her.

Alexa put one hand on the swing chain to stop it from moving. "Marya, are you listening?" she asked me. "This is going to be good. You better listen."

"Ugh," I said. Now that the swing had stopped, I couldn't pretend I was somewhere else anymore.

She wrinkled her nose at me. "Why do you have to be so weird?"

I opened my mouth to say that she was the weird one, but she wasn't even looking at me. She was riffling through the bunch of papers in her hand. They were pink envelopes with red hearts stamped all over the front. The invitations. She handed each one out like it was a precious gift. "This Saturday at noon sharp!" she said. "Don't be late. My mom likes to start things on time, because she's on the city council, you know."

Yes, we all knew that. Alexa told us at least once every week about her mom.

The other kids were totally excited.

"What sort of cake will you have, Alexa?" someone asked. At her last birthday, she'd had chocolate mousse cake with strawberry ganache.

"What games will we play?" another kid asked.

Alexa's eyes glittered. "The cake will be awesome!" she replied. "Probably blueberry, since it's my new favorite flavor."

"Oooh, yummy," said Hanna.

I glared at her. She was supposed to be my best friend. And she didn't even like blueberries. Why was she ooh-ing at Alexa's imaginary cake?

"And there will be lots of games," Alexa continued. "A bouncy house, and a waterslide, and maybe even a magic show!"

The kids clapped and hoorayed.

"That sounds ah-mazing!" Hanna almost screamed.

I scowled. This was ridiculous. Had Hanna forgotten it was my birthday this weekend too? Why was she making such a big deal about Alexa's party? Why was everyone?

Okay, I knew why. Because Alexa's parties were legendary. Everyone talked about them at school for days afterward.

I jumped off the swing. "It's my birthday too, you know," I said loudly.

Everyone quieted down. "Really?" Antonio asked, frowning like he didn't believe it. "Are you having a party too?"

Alexa turned her bright blue eyes on me. "Don't be silly. Marya doesn't do parties."

My mouth opened and closed. I'd never admit it, but she was right. The other kids started to walk away, whispering about Alexa's invitations.

When it was only Hanna and Alexa left, I found my voice. "I do too," I said weakly. "Parties, I mean."

Alexa pushed a pink envelope gently toward me. "It's okay, Marya. No need to make things up. Here's your invite. I hope you come! It will be fabulous!"

I grabbed the envelope from her. "I'm not making things up! I will have a fabulous party too!" I remembered the show Dadi was watching this morning. "There will be fairy lights and music and . . . and a fashion show."

Alexa's mouth dropped open. "A fashion show?"

I nodded very fast. "Yes, yes, that's right. And lots of yummy food. Tons of it, really."

Hanna pinched me on the arm. Her eyes were as big as the saucers that go with Mama's teacups. "What are you doing?" she whispered very loudly. "Your parents never let you have parties."

I moved away from her before she could pinch me again. "No, this is special. Mama and Baba will say yes."

Alexa crossed her arms over her chest and glared at me. "What else will you have?" she demanded.

I took a deep breath. *I should stop talking now,* I told myself. But it was too late. I'd already said too much. I tried to think about the girl on TV with her bright red clothes and the henna on her hands. She was so beautiful. I leaned forward. "And the best thing about my party," I said slowly, "will be . . . henna!"

Hanna and Alexa both went, "Ooooh."

I gulped. Nobody had ever oohed for me before. "Yes, that's right. It's a henna party." I

grinned so big I could feel my mouth stretch out. I bet Alexa had never had a henna party. Not in a million years.

"So where are your invites?" Alexa asked. Her arms were hanging by her sides now, and I could tell she wanted an invite to my henna party really badly.

I tried to keep a serious face. "Tomorrow," I promised. "I'll bring them tomorrow."

The bell rang for recess to be over, and everyone ran back to class. Alexa gave me a stare. Then she turned and went back to class too, clutching a few pink envelopes in her hands.

I smiled again, just in case she turned around and saw me.

4

WORD OF THE DAY

FORBIDDEN

Not permitted

or allowed

After school that day, Hanna and I headed outside to the pickup area at the front of the school. Pickup time was boring if you didn't have your bestie with you. All the kids had to stand according to grade level and watch for their cars. Teachers called the kids' names as their cars drove up. That meant you had to stay quiet so you could hear the names.

Nobody was ever quiet.

It was the perfect time to talk about my birthday party.

"You mean your imaginary party," Hanna said, laughing. "The one that doesn't actually exist."

"It does too," I replied. "Or at least, it could."

She sighed. "Why did you lie, Marya? Your parents think lying is the worst thing in the world."

Oh yeah. She was talking about that one time last year when I'd spilled juice over Baba's papers on his desk and then blamed Sal for it. Hanna had been at my house that day, so she'd heard the scolding I'd gotten from Baba. And Mama.

And Dadi. Not for the orange juice, but for lying about it.

Sal had totally deserved it, though. He'd been sneaking up on us all day as we played, taking our toys, shouting Boo! Was it my fault I decided to take some revenge?

"Lying's not really the worst thing," I told Hanna. "You know what's the worst thing? Alexa."

"Come on, she's not so bad."

I narrowed my eyes. "Yes, she is. You're just saying that because you want to go to her house this Saturday."

Hanna waved a hand in front of my face. "Just forget it. Tell me about this imaginary party of yours."

My eyes stayed narrowed for a few more seconds. Was she trying to change the subject so I'd forget how excited she'd been about the blueberry cake? Then I relaxed. "It will be fabulous!" I told her. "And it will be real, just as soon as I can convince my parents."

"And how are you going to do that?"

"Through my powers of persuasion," I told her. That was another one of my Word of the Day words, and it fit perfectly.

The only problem was, Hanna didn't have a Word of the Day diary like me. "You're going to wear perfume?" she asked, her eyebrows all scrunched up, confused.

I thought about a superstrong perfume that could make my parents do whatever I wanted. A magical potion. "That would be awesome," I sighed. "But no, that's not what I mean."

"Then what—?"

Beep! Beep!

I turned as Mama's van rumbled up. I could see Aliyah slumped in the front seat.

"MARYA KHAN! SALMAN KHAN!" a teacher yelled as she read the card on the van's windshield. I saw Sal move away from the fifth-grade line.

Hanna stomped her foot. "Marya, tell me what you're planning," she whined. "You always plan things that get us in trouble."

This was true. But it was also fun.

"I'll tell you later, alligator," I said as I hurried away behind Sal.

Mama dropped the three of us at home and sped away to her shop in that smelly van of hers. She usually didn't go back in the afternoon, but her assistant was sick this week. Or maybe he'd just gotten tired of the stinky fertilizer all around him.

"Don't forget to eat something," Mama shouted as she waved goodbye to us. "There's lots of food in the fridge!"

I waved back. "Don't worry, Aliyah can help me get some snacks."

Aliyah slammed the door behind us and dropped her backpack in the hallway. "Not happening," she growled, stomping away to the living room.

"What's your problem?" I shouted after her. Actually, I didn't want to know. Ever since she'd started middle school, there was always some drama going on in her life.

Sal was already in the kitchen, his head stuck in the fridge. "We have daal and yogurt and apples . . ." he called out.

I grabbed a bag of chips and headed to my room while he was still talking. What did I care about my big sister? She hardly ever spent time with me anyway. She had her own life, and I had mine. And right now, I had some planning to do.

I had to convince my parents to let me have the best party in the world. That would need more than just words. I would have to show them. An example, like Miss Piccolo always said.

Aha! A picture!

I shut my bedroom door and found some paper and pens on my desk. Perfect! I climbed on my bed and lay on my stomach, eyes closed, imagining the scene from Dadi's show. Trees with fairy lights. A band playing guitars. A table full of food. Pitchers of juice and tea. Finally, I opened my eyes and started to sketch on the paper, my hands moving quickly. Even though I wasn't great at art, the scene looked okay.

On top, I wrote MARYA'S HENNA PARTY!! in pretty block letters. My art may be so-so, but my handwriting was the best in third grade.

I turned the paper over and traced my hand, palm up. That's where my henna design would go. Only I didn't really know how to draw those.

Aliyah! I remembered that she had a book of henna designs in her room somewhere. It was big and bright yellow, like one of those coffee table books at Hanna's house. Aliyah loved making henna designs on our little cousins' hands on Eid. All I needed to do was sneak into her room and find the book without being seen.

I gulped. Entering Aliyah's room was strictly forbidden. There was even a huge sign on the door saying exactly that: *Entry Strictly Forbidden.*

Still, I needed that book, or my sketch wouldn't be complete. Before I could chicken out, I scrambled off my bed and ran to her room, just across from mine. I opened the door slowly. Carefully. It was empty. And dark. Aliyah was probably still downstairs.

I switched on the light and headed to her bookshelf. No henna book. I looked around. Her desk had a bunch of papers and pens scattered about. Her floor was even worse, piled high with clothes and shoes. I couldn't see an inch of actual carpet.

Ugh. Even if the book was here, I'd never find it.

"Marya, Mama's on the phone!" came Aliyah's voice from through the door. Yikes, she was coming up the stairs. I panicked and ran toward the door. Just before I left, I saw something yellow peeking out from under her bed. Yes! I grabbed the book lightning fast, then ran back to my room like witches were after me.

Or just Aliyah. Same thing.

5

WORD OF THE DAY

PERSUASION

Making someone

do or believe

something

I decided that the most likely person to fall under my persuasion spell was Baba. He was my favorite person in the whole family, mostly because he always took my side when I got into trouble.

Well, except when I spilled that juice on his papers.

When he came home from work, I opened the door for him, holding my sketch behind my back. "Salaam, Baba," I said with a big smile. It wasn't even a lie. I was always happy to see him.

"Salaam, my little girl," he said, kissing me on the forehead. He put away his shoes in the hallway closet and went into the living room.

I followed him like a puppy. Well, except my tongue wasn't hanging out. That would be weird.

Baba stretched out on the couch, yawning.

I sat down next to him and put my sketch on the floor. Then I smiled again, right at him.

He looked at me. "Do you need something, my love?"

I smiled wider. He always called me his love. I shook my head and snuggled up to him. "Why would I need something?" I asked.

He sighed and pinched his nose with his fingers. "Out with it, Marya. What do you want?"

I stopped smiling. "Well . . ."

He looked at me with his soft brown eyes. "I knew it! Come on, tell me. Is it about your birthday? I know it's coming up. I have the most awesome present for you."

My ears tingled. "You do? What is it?"

He shook his head. "Can't tell you. It's a surprise."

I was practically *dying* to guess the surprise, but I made myself stop. This was not the time to talk about presents. "Baba, I was wondering . . ."

"Yes?"

"Can I have a party this year?" I said very fast. "For my birthday?"

He frowned. "We're already having a party, aren't we? We'll all be together, your mama and me, and Dadi—"

I cut in. "I meant a big party. For my friends. With pretty invitations and everything."

He frowned some more. His smile was completely gone by now. I didn't like that. "You're inviting Hanna, aren't you? She's your best friend."

I wanted to stomp my foot, but I didn't think that would make Baba's smile come back. "No, all my friends. Everyone in the class." I picked the sketch up from the floor and pushed it at him, breathing hard. "I want a birthday party with music and food and games, and a magic show! Why can't I have a magic show?"

He stared at the paper like he couldn't understand it. "What is this? A magic show? Have you lost your mind, my love?" He looked at me and took a deep breath. "We can't do this, Marya, I'm sorry. Big parties cost a lot of money."

I was still breathing hard. Did Baba just say no to me? I couldn't remember the last time he'd said no to me. I made big puppy-dog eyes. That always worked with him. "Baba, please? I need this party so bad! I'm going to be eight years old. It's a big deal."

He handed me the sketch. "Eight years old? Amazing! Come, let's watch some cartoons together, eh?" He hugged me. "You'll have a great birthday with your family and best friend. And I hear Mama's going to bake you a delicious chocolate cake!"

I pulled away from his hug. "I wanted blueberries," I told him.

Actually, I hissed.

And then I ran away to my room before Baba could reply.

Since my powers hadn't worked on Baba, I decided to try his mom instead. In the evening, I brought my sketch to the dinner table and showed it to Dadi while we waited for dinner. Sal and Aliyah were helping Mama with dinner prep . . . or at least they were supposed to be.

"It's your turn to set the plates," Sal said loudly.

"No, I'm making the salad," Aliyah replied. "You set the plates."

"Kids, please! Stop arguing!" Baba told both of them with a frown. He was ladling spaghetti into a big bowl while Mama made roti on the stove.

The spaghetti was for me. I didn't like eating roti too much.

I turned to Dadi with my sketch. "Wouldn't this be great for my birthday?" I whispered.

Dadi smiled and inspected my drawing. "Very pretty," she finally said. "Just like my TV show."

"Yes." I nodded very fast. "I want—"

Too late. Dadi was already talking about her show. "That girl turned out to be a detective, you know. There was a thief at the party who stole all the good presents, and she figured out who it was. Do you know who the thief was?"

I shook my head sadly. "No, I don't," I said, pushing my sketch away. It was no use. Nobody was paying attention to me. As usual.

Dadi smacked her hand on the table. "The schoolteacher, that's who. It was totally unexpected! You should have seen my face—"

Aliyah came up to us with her salad bowl. "What's this?" she asked, peering at my sketch. "Did you draw this, Marya?"

"Yes, she did, isn't it wonderful?" Dadi said, beaming. "Marya wants a birthday party just like the girl on my show."

Aliyah laughed. "Oh em gee this is so over the top. A band? Really?"

"Shut up," I muttered. I wished I'd never made that sketch.

Aliyah didn't stop. Instead, she got even louder. "What's gotten into you, Marya? I'm a teenager and even I'd never get a party like this."

Sal laughed too. "Yeah, me neither."

Ugh. What did I do to deserve these two? I grabbed my sketch. "Forget it," I told them through tight lips. "You won't understand."

Baba shushed them both with a finger. "Be nice to your sister, please."

I felt a tiny bit better. Then Mama came over and patted my head like I was a baby. "Come now, eat some spaghetti and forget all this nonsense."

My shoulders slumped. Nobody cared that Alexa R. was having a way cooler birthday than me.

6

WORD OF THE DAY

RECIPROCATE

To return

a favor

bviously, Alexa was waiting for me at recess the next day. "Well?" she demanded, hands on her hips. She was wearing another dress. It was navy blue with tiny rainbows all over. Oh, and lots of lace. What was even the point of wearing lace in the school playground? Didn't she see all the mud on the ground?

Alexa said "Well?" again.

I acted like I had no idea what she was talking about. "Well what?" I said, looking around. The swings were already taken, so I had nowhere to

go. I glared at the kids who were swinging away like they had nothing to worry about.

Alexa snapped her fingers in front of my face. "Well, where are your invitations?" she asked.

"What invitations?"

"Marya Khan, are you being mean on purpose?" Alexa asked, her voice high like she'd swallowed the air from a balloon. Which she'll probably have a bunch of at her party on Saturday.

I looked at her, shocked. "Mean? I'm never mean."

"I invite you to my birthday party every year. Every single year. Don't I?"

I nodded, looking at the ground. It was true. I'd been going to her annoying parties ever since I could remember. I figured she invited me because we were neighbors, and her mom made her. "So?"

She sighed like I was a complete doofus. "So now it's your turn. I want to come to your henna party. It sounds amazing."

I bit my lip. I couldn't tell her I'd made it all up, could I?

Dadi always said I should tell the truth, even if I'd made a bad mistake. Dadi would be really mad at me right now.

Wait a minute. Was this really a mistake? My birthday wasn't for almost a whole week. I could still have a party. I could convince Mama. She always listened to me when she was in a good mood. I decided to try my powers of persuasion one more time, today, after school.

But Alexa was waiting for her invitation. Why did I have to say all those things yesterday?

"Listen, Alexa," I said in a whisper. "I have a secret."

She leaned forward, very alert. She was like a deer I saw in my aunt's backyard in Minnesota one time. "What is it?"

"I still have to ask my mom about the party. So can you . . . maybe . . . not talk about it to everyone? Please?"

Her eyes grew round. "So, it's a private party, huh? Just for a few kids? Special?"

What was she even talking about? "I guess," I finally replied.

She rubbed her hands together. "Perfect. My lips are sealed."

But she was grinning with her mouth wide open, so I'm not sure what she meant.

Mama picked me up early from school because I had a dentist appointment. It was just a regular cleaning, so no big deal. Hanna hated dentists, but I thought they were pretty cool. Making people's teeth all pretty and clean, and getting rid of all the germs? It's the perfect job.

Plus, our dentist, Dr. Wong, always gave me a bunch of presents in a little baggie after I was done with my cleaning. I said thank you to him and looked into the baggie while Mama paid in the front office. A small toothpaste, a pink toothbrush, three stickers of My Little Pony, and one plastic bracelet that lit up when you shook it. I put it on my wrist at once. Hanna would be so surprised to see it.

"Can we stop by the Pakistani store on our way back?" Mama asked when we got into her van. I really didn't want to because I was starving, but I nodded because of two very important reasons. One, the van was clean of all the usual bags of poop—sorry, fertilizer—so I was happy. Second, I decided that giving Mama what she wanted would put her in a good mood and give me what I wanted: a henna party. According to my Word of the Day diary, that's called reciprocation.

Oh, and there's a third reason too. The Pakistani store is pretty awesome.

❀

"Can I have some spicy chips?" I asked Mama as we went inside. It wasn't my fault. They had a big display of snacks in the front of the shop, just waiting for hungry kids to see when they came in.

Mama pulled me away from the display. "You just got your teeth cleaned, remember?"

"So?" I scowled, turning my head to look at the chips. "Does that mean I can never eat again?"

She gave me a little smile. "Okay fine, go get a bag. I'll tell the owner we'll pay for it with the rest of our things."

I grinned back and did what she said. Seemed like Mama was in a listening mood today.

She signaled to the shopkeeper and grabbed a cart. We walked through the store together, me munching on my chips and Mama going through her grocery list on her phone. We had a shopping system: She called out the things she needed, and I grabbed them.

"Rice," she called out.

I picked up the brand she liked, the one with a zebra on the front.

"Garlic and ginger paste."

I got the big bottle because I knew she put that yucky stuff in everything she cooked.

Then I saw something amazing. Something beautiful, right in front of me like a giant sign from the universe.

A tall display rack of henna cones.

"Daal," Mama said, but I wasn't paying attention. My eyes were glued to the henna cones.

"Perfect," I whispered, inching closer.

"What?" Mama asked. "Daal is the other way, Marya."

I reached the henna cones and touched them with gentle fingers. "Mama, please can we have a henna party this Sunday?" I whispered.

Mama wheeled the cart away from me quickly. "Marya! For the last time, we're not having a big party."

I opened my mouth to argue, but she was already halfway to the daal section. Maybe it wasn't the best idea to spring this on Mama. She got very focused when she was shopping. Which was totally unfair because she should be focused on me right now. To reciprocate.

I crossed my arms over my chest and followed her. Mama shopped some more, but I didn't talk to her again. She paid for everything and we got back to her van.

I guess she must have figured out I was mad at her, because instead of turning the key, she turned and looked at me. "Listen, Marya. I'm sorry, but we just can't, okay?"

I kept my arms crossed. "Why not?" If she talked about how much parties cost, I'd scream. I bet Alexa never had to worry about money.

"It's too late to plan anything big," Mama said. "Besides, I'm working this weekend, remember?"

Oh yeah, the big wedding. My heart dropped into my stomach.

So basically, I wasn't getting my henna party because of poop fertilizer.

WORD OF THE DAY

OPERATION

A set of plans

to achieve

a goal

inner that night was more like a circus. Except circus animals are cute and know lots of tricks. My family is the opposite of cute, and they know exactly zero tricks. Mama kept forgetting to turn over the roti in the skillet and burned three of them. Sal dropped a plate on the floor and Baba made him clean it up. My

brother howled about that for ten straight minutes. I know, because I counted.

Sixty times ten. That's ten minutes.

"Okay, listen up!" Mama said when we finally started eating. "The rest of this week is really busy for me because of my client's wedding. I need you kids to step up."

"Baba can be in charge." Sal grinned with food in his mouth. Ew.

Aliyah rolled her eyes. "You're just saying that because Baba lets you play video games all day."

"Video games are good for you," Sal told her. "They teach you valuable lessons—"

"No video games!" Mama interrupted, giving Baba a stern look. "Sal, you have that math test to study for."

Sal groaned.

"And Aliyah has to clean her room. It's a pigsty."

"It is not!" Aliyah said, huffing.

Mama was right. I'd been inside Aliyah's room. Even pigs would refuse to live there.

I kept my head down and ate my roti. There

was no spaghetti today, but I kept quiet. Mama didn't say anything to me. I guess she thought I was still mad.

But I wasn't mad anymore. I was thinking very hard. I closed my eyes and imagined my party sketch with the henna hand on the back. I could still make that happen. I just had to come up with a good plan.

Mama was still talking. "This wedding is very important to me. It's a big client and they expect everything to be perfect. So, I can't afford to get distracted."

"Don't worry," Baba said, giving her a sideways hug. "You won't."

Then Mama said something that made me open my eyes and listen very carefully. "I'll need all the help I can get at home."

I almost jumped up from my chair. That was it! That's how I'd get my henna party! I'd help Mama and Baba—and maybe even Aliyah and

Sal—so much this week that they'd be speech- less. And then they'd ask me what I wanted in return, and I'd say, "Nothing, except maybe a fancy schmancy henna party. With music. And an elephant."

Baba frowned at me. "Elephant? What are you talking about?"

Oops. I think I said that last part out loud. "Nothing," I replied quickly. "I meant an elephant toy, for Alexa's birthday."

Mama groaned so loudly that everyone turned to look at her in surprise. "Alexa's birthday!" she said. "We haven't gotten her a gift yet!"

Baba held up a hand. "No problem. I'll do it."

"You will?" Mama and I said together.

He nodded firmly. "Yes. I'll take Marya shop- ping on Saturday morning and she can find this elephant toy she wants for Alexa."

I couldn't decide what to say. Did they even have elephant toys for eight-year-old girls who dressed like every day was a party? Then I shrugged and settled back in my chair. I had bigger things to worry about.

I had to make a plan.

❊

"So, what's your plan?" Hanna asked me the next day. Alexa was absent, so we had our table-square all to ourselves. It was like being in heaven.

"Operation Help the Khans," I told her.

She looked totally confused, so I explained my idea. How I'd help everyone at home with their chores, and they'd reward me for being such a kind person by fulfilling all my dreams.

Aka the henna party.

"You don't even like being teacher's helper in class," Hanna protested.

That was only because Miss Piccolo had the most boring jobs for us, like organizing the classroom library in alphabetical order or taking the recycling to the front office. "This is different," I replied. "This will be grand."

It was the biggest, bestest plan of all. Mama

and Baba were always complaining that nobody helped around the house. Well, that would change soon, thanks to Marya Khan the Amazing Helper.

When we got home after school (this time in Baba's nice car instead of the stinky van), I followed Aliyah up the stairs. "Mama told you to clean your room, remember?"

Aliyah gave me a thunderous look. "Go away, it's none of your business."

I smiled very sweetly. "I know. But I can help you. We'll get it done in no time."

She stopped in her tracks. "Why? What's going on?"

I tried to look innocent. "Nothing. I just think we should help Mama more, you know? She does everything around the house and she's got the shop too."

Aliyah started toward the bathroom in the hallway. "I guess," she said, her voice no longer mad. "But I don't need you poking around in my room. I'll clean it myself."

I watched as she disappeared in the bathroom and slammed the door shut. Yeah, right. She'd never do it by herself.

"I'm going to help you, okay?" I shouted.

"Go away!" she shouted back.

She didn't really mean it. She'd be so grateful if I helped her. I went into her room and started cleaning up. I picked up her clothes from the floor and sniffed them. They were a bit funky, but I hung them in her closet anyway. I stacked all her books in a neat pile on her desk, even the henna design book I'd borrowed earlier. Then I turned to her vanity. Hairbrushes and bracelets were strewn all over. I picked up a tiny glass bottle of perfume. It said *Joyful Jasmine* on the label.

"I told you I didn't need help!" came a very Aliyah-sounding shriek from the door.

I gasped and whirled around. The glass bottle fell from my hand and shattered. A trickle of liquid smelling very strongly of jasmine spread across the table.

Oops.

"What are you doing?" Aliyah's shriek grew louder and more piercing.

My hand trembled as I tried to clean up the glass. "I'm sorry, it's not my fault. You scared me!"

Aliyah pulled me up by my arm and pushed me toward the door. "Leave! Leave!" she screamed.

I ran to my room. I sat on my bed and took deep breaths. Maybe starting Operation Help the Khans with the worst Khan of the family hadn't been such a great idea.

8

WORD OF THE DAY

FAILURE

When something

doesn't work out

the way it should

My next target was Sal. I found my brother eating a giant chicken and cheese sandwich on the living room floor next to a pile of LEGO bricks. "What're you doing?" I asked, sitting down next to him.

"Eating," he replied. "Want some?"

I looked around, but there were no other sandwiches nearby. Was he talking about the disgusting mess in his hands? "Er, no thanks," I said.

He turned back to his LEGO project. It was a half-built spaceship of some kind, with big wings and a silver cockpit. "Don't touch anything," he warned me.

I narrowed my eyes. "Don't you have a math test to study for?" I demanded.

He looked up. "What are you, a spy?"

"Mama was talking about it at dinner last night. You should go study. Don't you want her to be happy with you?"

Sal stuffed the last of his sandwich into his mouth. "RRRRRRRR."

"What?"

He swallowed. "I said, I'll do it later."

I gave him my best glare. "You should do it now. Before Mama gets home." I stopped, thinking how I could make him listen. "Otherwise . . ."

He stood up so quickly, crumbs flew out in all directions. "Okay, okay, don't tell Mama. I'm going to study."

I grinned as he left. Then I turned around to look at his LEGO spaceship. It was big and ugly and had gaping holes where Sal still hadn't put in LEGOs. My grin got wider. I was getting another great idea. I'd make his spaceship for him while he studied. He'd be so happy with me! Maybe he'd even tell Mama and Baba what a good sister I was.

I got to work. It wasn't hard. I looked at the instruction manual and followed it step-by-step. Step-by-step.

After a few minutes, I stopped. Was there supposed to be a red arch in the middle of the black ship? It looked strange. I turned it around, but then it looked even worse. I reached over and flipped the pages of the manual. Oops! I'd missed two pages!

I stared at the thing in my hand. It didn't look like a spaceship anymore. It looked more like a monster with wings. And a red arch. Oh no!

I put the spaceship down and got up from the floor quickly. If Sal came back and found me

messing with his LEGOs, he'd scream just like Aliyah had. They never liked it when I touched their stuff.

The house was very quiet. It felt nice. I went to the kitchen and got some strawberries from the fridge. Strawberries were my favorite fruit, but I liked bananas too. If you mixed up these two fruits in Greek yogurt and added a little honey, they made the best after-school snack in the world.

I ate slowly at the kitchen counter and thought about Day 1 of Operation Help the Khans. I hadn't done the best job, but at least it was something.

I was showing my family that I could be helpful and kind. So what if things sometimes got a little messed up?

Okay, a lot messed up.

I'd almost finished eating when I heard Sal come downstairs. Oh no! He was going to find his monster spaceship any minute now. I stood up quickly and ran to Dadi's room.

Dadi lay snuggled under the covers in her bed, snoring loudly. Her gray hair was spread untidily on her pillow. When I was little, I used to be scared of Dadi's snores. Petrified, according to my Word of the Day diary. But now I was big and not easily scared.

Besides, the snores meant she was fast asleep. Which meant I could do something helpful without her finding out. I grinned. I could be like the little elves who came into the shoemaker's shop and fixed all the shoes in the middle of the night.

Now I only needed to find out what needed fixing.

I peeked into Dadi's closet. It was neat as a pin.

I checked her dresser. Everything was arranged very nicely. Not a comb was out of place.

Then I crawled under her bed. Bingo! It was full of junk. There were dusty boxes and stacks of Urdu magazines. I could clean this all for her and she'd be so happy with me! And then she'd tell Mama to give me the big party. Dadi was an elder, and she was Mama's mother-in-law. Mama had to do what Dadi said.

Didn't she?

I told myself to focus, and got to work. I pulled out a box and sat on the floor cross-legged. It was full of papers and other things. I cleaned everything with the edge of my shirt and put it back neatly. There was so much dust I had to wrinkle my nose to stop from sneezing.

A glint of light caught my eye. It was a pearl necklace. I took it out of the box and stared at it. Were those real pearls? I'd never seen Dadi wear jewelry like this.

ACHOO!

I sneezed, and Dadi stopped snoring. Oops!

"What are you doing, Marya?" Dadi's voice was drowsy but also a little bit mad.

I gulped. Dadi never got mad at me.

"I . . . I'm sorry. I was trying to clean up . . ."

Dadi got out of her bed and snatched the necklace from my hands. "You shouldn't go through other people's private things!" she said. She stood over me, her bare feet just inches from my crossed legs.

I sneezed again. "I'm sorry," I repeated. I couldn't believe Dadi was mad about a dusty old box. "I was only trying to help!"

She glared at me. "Help? I don't need help. You have to ask people's permission before helping them."

I looked down at her feet. Was that true? Did you need someone's permission to help them? It didn't make a lot of sense to me.

I stood up, trying not to cry. "Okay, I'll go now." I thought she'd stop me and offer to put on another Pakistani drama. But Dadi only looked at me angrily, clutching the necklace to her chest.

I bit my lip and left the room. Operation Help the Khans was a big, fat failure.

WORD OF THE DAY

Food baked

together and served

in a deep dish

hat are you going to do now?" Hanna asked at recess the next day. We were sitting on a wooden bench on the edge of the playground, watching the other kids play. Alexa was standing near the swings, talking to a bunch of girls. Probably describing her gorgeous party this weekend.

Which was only two days away.

I wanted to scream and throw something. But I didn't. That would only get me in trouble. I squared my shoulders and turned away from Alexa. "I have one last idea," I replied.

"Forget about the entire thing?" Hanna suggested.

I scowled at her. "Don't you want a fabulous henna party?"

She shrugged. "Not really. I like our regular birthday parties. Pizza and cake and movie night. That's how we've always done it, and it's fun."

I scowled some more. How could she think boring old pizza and cake was more fun than a dazzling big party? "Whose side are you on?" I demanded.

She patted my arm. "I'm on your side. If you want a band and an elephant on your birthday, I'm happy with that too."

I relaxed. "Good."

She giggled. "Can you imagine? The elephant would stomp all over the stage and knock over the band's equipment."

I stopped scowling and smiled a little. "No elephant," I promised. Then I remembered what had happened at dinner two nights ago. "I may have to get a toy one for Alexa, though."

She giggled some more. "She'll be so shocked."

I looked back at Queen Alexa, surrounded by her subjects. "Good," I muttered.

When recess ended, Alexa was waiting for me by the classroom door. "Can't wait for your party!" she whispered in my ear, like it was a big secret.

Oh right. I'd told her it was a secret so she wouldn't tell everyone else.

I made my lips curve into a smile. "Sure!" I whispered back. "Can't wait."

After school, I got ready to put the last part of my plan into action. It required being completely alone.

I checked on every member of the family. Aliyah and Sal were in their rooms, after telling me to stay away from their stuff. "You're dangerous," Aliyah said, jabbing a finger at me.

I had no idea what she was talking about.

Dadi was snoring away in her room. Mama was in her shop as usual. Baba was working from home, but the door to his office was closed and I could hear him talking loudly to someone on the phone.

Perfect.

I headed to the kitchen and put on Mama's apron that hung behind the pantry door. It was too long, and I thought about cutting the hem.

Then I decided Mama would probably not approve. I let it hang to my ankles and got to work. I took out all the things I needed. A baking dish. A mixing bowl. A can of soup. Cheese. Butter. Breadcrumbs. Mixed vegetables from the freezer. Salt and pepper. The pantry had other spices like ground cumin and rosemary. I decided to use those as well.

I was going to cook dinner tonight.

I was going to make a vegetable casserole. No, it wasn't the typical Pakistani food that Dadi liked, but everyone else in the family would love it. And Mama would be so happy to come home from her flower shop and find a delicious, warm dinner already on the table.

I would be the hero! And I would ask for my henna party as a reward for my heroism.

I didn't need my Word of the Day diary to tell me what heroism meant. All I needed was to look in the mirror.

Now to get cooking. I tightened the apron around my waist and looked at the stuff piled in front of me. My hand trembled a little bit, but I smacked it down on the counter. It was no big deal. I'd helped Mama make casseroles dozens of times. This was going to be fabulous.

I emptied out the frozen veggies into the baking dish. Did Mama usually cook them first? I couldn't remember. They looked okay, I decided. I used Baba's electric can opener to open the soup—cream of mushroom, yummy!—and poured

it all over the veggies in a circle pattern. Then I added a cup of cheese, but it looked too little, so I dumped the whole packet in. You could never have too much cheese, right?

I sprinkled salt, pepper, cumin, and rosemary over everything. I was an expert at sprinkling spices.

I grabbed the mixing bowl next. Mama and I made brownie batter in it on weekends. I mixed together butter and breadcrumbs and spread it over the veggies. Then I put on oven mitts and opened the oven door.

To be honest, I wasn't really supposed to touch a hot oven. But this was a special situation, so I decided it was okay. The oven wasn't even hot. I put the baking dish inside and closed the door.

I cleaned up the counter and put away the apron. I couldn't remember how long the casserole should cook, so I decided to let Mama handle that part. She'd be home soon anyway.

I was almost up to my room when I realized I hadn't even put the oven on.

Yikes! I ran back downstairs and set the oven to 350 degrees. That's what we always did for brownies, anyway.

Now to wait.

And wait. And wait.

In the meantime, I drew some more sketches of my henna party. This time I drew myself and all my friends too, eating and dancing, and having fun. Alexa stood in the corner of my drawing,

watching us. Her dress was fancy and pretty, but so was mine. It was the red shalwar kameez the girl in Dadi's Pakistani drama was wearing.

❦

I must have fallen asleep on my bed. The next thing I knew, a piercing BEEEEEEP woke me up. Mama was shouting "FIRE!" from downstairs. I opened my eyes and looked at the sky from my window. It was evening, which meant Mama was home and dinner was ready.

Dinner.

My casserole?

That's when I noticed the smell of smoke. Oh no! The oven!

I slid off of my bed and rushed downstairs. Aliyah rushed out of her room at the same time. "What did you do now, Marya?" she shrieked.

I wanted to say "nothing," but this time, I wasn't sure. My heart was thumping so hard it felt like a drum in my chest. I raced Aliyah to the kitchen.

The oven was open, and smoke was pouring out. Mama had the oven mitts on, clutching a

dark brown baking dish in her hands. Yes, it was definitely the casserole. I'd forgotten to tell Mama about it. Baba, Sal, and Dadi all peered into the dish like it was a big pot of poop fertilizer. On fire.

Everyone was shouting. At me.

My heart stopped thumping and sank to my toes. Operation Help the Khans was officially over.

10

WORD OF THE DAY

SPECTACULAR

Causing wonder

and admiration

Knock-knock-knock!

Ugh. I didn't want to wake up on Saturday morning. Really, was it too much to let a girl sleep in on the weekend?

"Come on, Marya," Baba called from outside my door. "We have to go buy Alexa's gift before heading to her place."

Ugh. Alexa. Why was she always in my life? Why couldn't she live somewhere else instead of right next door?

Baba knocked again.

"I'm coming!" I called out.

Then I stayed in bed for another ten minutes. When I finally dragged myself up, it was almost ten in the morning. I put on the only dress I had, a denim one with long sleeves, and sparkly white leggings.

Alexa's party invitations said twelve o'clock sharp. What did *sharp* have to do with the time, anyway?

Baba was waiting for me in the kitchen with a plate of French toast with maple syrup. "Mama's already left for the shop," he told me. "I'll take you wherever you need to go today."

I sniffed. "Thanks, Baba," I said quietly. French toast was usually my favorite, but I didn't feel like eating anything right then.

Nobody had spoken to me much since

Thursday evening. Aliyah and Sal had insisted I get punished for almost burning down the house, but Mama had hugged me and said she understood I was only trying to help. "Your heart's in the right place, jaan," she'd said when she tucked me in at bedtime. "You just don't think before doing things sometimes."

I'd looked at Mama in the light of my lamp. She looked tired. She'd been working overtime at her flower shop all week to prepare for the big wedding. "Thinking is overrated," I told her, rolling my eyes.

She'd ruffled my hair and smiled. "Thinking before you do something is what growing up is all about," she said. "Remember that next time."

I'd spent all of Friday thinking. Racking my brains, really, to come up with a new plan for my party. I'd come up with exactly zero. I think my brain cells got fried along with the casserole.

Now, in the kitchen, I ate a few bites of my French toast while Baba checked his emails on his phone. "Ready?" he finally asked.

I nodded. I wasn't ready, but nobody really cared about how I felt, anyway.

"So, what sort of present do you want to get for your friend?" he asked me in the car.

I shrugged. "I don't know. Something with animals?" I'd been kidding about the elephant, but I knew Alexa liked animals. A lot. Her family had three cats and a dog.

Baba took me downtown. We dropped in at Mama's shop to say hi, but she hardly looked up. Her shop was so full of flowers, you couldn't

even see the floor. Mama gave us a hurried smile. "Salaam! It's the big day today!"

I glared at her because I thought she was talking about Alexa's party. Then I remembered. "Oh, the wedding. Good luck!"

She wasn't even paying attention anymore.

Baba dragged me away to the shop next door called Kids Korner. It had kids' furniture and things you could put in your room. I looked around, trying to imagine what Alexa would like.

"How about this?" Baba asked, and I turned. He was holding a little porcelain piggy bank in the shape of a pink elephant.

"Perfect!" I cried.

✤

Alexa's house was next door to ours, but it was twice as big. I clutched Baba's hand tightly as we walked up to her front yard. There was a big wooden number 8 standing in the grass, with colorful balloons attached to it. A black truck stood on the street, with the words *Wizard Caiden's Magical Journey* written on the side with gold paint.

This was the famous magic show Alexa had promised.

I wanted to stomp my foot and scream. I

hadn't even gone inside and already this party was spectacular.

"It'll be fun," Baba told me. "Just relax."

"Yeah, right," I muttered.

The front door was open. "Hi, Marya!" I saw Hanna waving from inside.

I hugged Baba goodbye and went in. There were so many people already there. My entire class, plus some of their parents. Everyone was smiling really big. Everyone except me.

I stood next to Hanna and looked around. Alexa's house was so fancy. The windows had golden curtains, and the floor was made of shiny black marble. And the furniture was . . . very straight and wooden, like in a museum. I'm not sure how Alexa and her three cats and one dog really lived here. It looked like a painting, not a real house.

"Where's Alexa?" I asked Hanna.

She shrugged. "I don't know. I haven't seen her. Not her mom and dad either."

I pointed to the backyard, where I could see a

swimming pool and a bouncy house. And more kids. "Maybe she's out there." Obviously, if I had a swimming pool, I'd spend all my time outside. Even at night.

A man in a long gown and a pointy purple hat came over and told us to go outside. He was holding a giant magic wand in his hands. I looked at him closely. It was Mr. Trenton, our neighbor. Mama once told me he was a writer, but all I knew was that he sat on his front porch every

day complaining about cars driving too fast. "Mr. Trenton?" I asked, just to make sure. Magic tricks didn't really seem like his thing.

The man shook his head and winked. "Call me Wizard Caiden," he replied, waving the wand right in front of my face.

We went outside through the big patio doors. "The show starts in fifteen minutes," said Wizard Caiden/Mr. Trenton. I wondered what tricks he knew. How to write a book without moving a muscle? How to make neighbors disappear?

"Ooh, cake!" Hanna whispered, and marched to a table full of food.

My eyes almost popped out of my head. There was so much food on this table. Fruit platters. Cheese cubes in big piles. Pastries and croissants. There was even a chocolate fountain.

This was . . . too much. It was like a party for adults, not a kid who'd just turned eight.

Suddenly, I realized pizza was a pretty good food for a party. And that my angry feelings were slowly going away.

I was still clutching Alexa's gift. I went over to the gift table and put my little box with the

elephant piggy bank next to all the giant boxes. I looked at the biggest box, wrapped in blue and silver paper. There was a card on the bow. "*For my darling Alexa. Sorry I couldn't be there in person. Love, Dad.*"

Wait a minute? Her dad wasn't at the party? How was that possible? Where was he?

I frowned. I couldn't imagine Baba not being there for my birthday. Or Mama or Dadi. Even Aliyah and Sal would never just . . . not show up.

Alexa must be feeling terrible.

I looked around.

Where *was* Alexa?

WORD OF THE DAY

SHATTERED

Broken into

small pieces

arya, are you coming?" Hanna called. "The magic show is starting soon."

"One minute." I left the gift table and started walking around the backyard. I saw a lot of kids—and adults—but no Alexa. This was her party. Where was she?

I went back inside the house. It was so quiet after the noises outside. I saw a plate of Oreos sitting on the kitchen counter and took one. Oreos were something Alexa and I both liked. One time, she'd brought a box of the double-cream ones to school and we ate all of it at recess.

The stomachache was totally worth it.

A phone rang loudly near my ear. I looked around. There was a big home phone with an answering machine near the fridge. It rang three times, then beeped.

"Hello darling, it's Mom. I'm sorry, I'm going to be late. There's been an emergency meeting of the city council and I have to be here. It's my job, you know. I'm sorry, but don't worry, Aunt Maryann will stay until I get back."

BEEP!

My mouth hung open. Did Alexa's mom just leave a message saying she couldn't come to her own daughter's party? This was horrible. First Alexa's dad, now her mom? What was even happening?

I gulped. That was a really important message. And I was the only one who'd heard it. I had to find Alexa and tell her.

Only I didn't really want to be the one who told her this bad news.

I took another Oreo, just to calm myself. Why did I even come inside the house? Why did I have to hear the message?

Then I heard a deep sigh, like someone was trying not to cry. I looked around. At the far end of the living room, behind a big leather couch, I saw a splash of bright green lace.

There was only one person I knew who wore lace. Alexa.

I walked over to the couch and peered behind it.

She was sitting on the floor, her knees drawn to her chest. And her face was very sad.

I didn't even think. I sat down next to her. "Are you okay, Alexa?" I whispered.

"I guess you heard the message, huh?" she whispered back.

I thought about lying, but I decided not to. I nodded. "Yup." Then I thought maybe I wasn't supposed to hear it. "I'm sorry, I was looking for you and—"

"It's okay. It's not your fault."

I looked at her in shock. She was being very nice. Was it because she was sad? Her face was wet, and her arms were tight around her knees. "Don't worry," I said. "Your mom will be here soon. And your aunt Maryann is pretty cool."

That was true. I'd met Alexa's aunt a lot of

times. Basically, whenever Alexa's mom or dad weren't around, her aunt babysat her.

Come to think of it, Aunt Maryann did a lot of babysitting for Alexa. Once, she even came for parent-teacher conferences at the school. I saw her holding Alexa's hand as they waited outside one of the classrooms. Alexa had the same sad look on her face.

I pulled my face into a grin. "Hey, Alexa, your party is awesome!"

Wow, those are words I never thought I'd say.

She shrugged. "It's okay."

"Okay? Are you kidding?" I pointed toward the front door. "There's a truck with a magical journey right outside!"

"Wizards scare me," she replied sadly.

I laughed.

"I'm serious. Those pointy hats and round glasses? No thanks!"

I rolled my eyes at her. I was starting to get a little bit mad. "Really? That's all you have to say? I guess you don't know how lucky you are. I've been trying to get my mama and baba to throw me a cool party and they keep saying no! I even helped them with a hundred things, and they still said no!"

She looked up at me. "What things?"

I suddenly thought of the burned casserole and Aliyah's broken perfume bottle. Only according to my Word of the Day diary, that would be a *shattered* bottle. And I thought of Dadi's angry face as I tried to clean her precious necklace. "It doesn't matter," I said. "Nobody wanted my help."

"I know how you feel." She frowned. "So, wait, the henna party isn't really happening?"

I shook my head slowly. Now I felt just as sad as Alexa. "Not happening," I repeated. It was the truth. I'd tried everything. I had no more plans.

I had failed.

We both sat behind the couch for a long time. I could hear kids laughing and screaming outside. I guess Mr. Trenton was a pretty good magician after all. It was weird to just sit there with Alexa, but it was also not weird. Mostly I thought about Operation Help the Khans and how I'd failed.

I'm pretty sure Alexa was thinking about her mom and dad not being at her birthday party. I decided that was way worse. I could always have my henna party next year.

"Alexa, cake!" Aunt Maryann called from the kitchen.

Alexa wiped her face, then stood up and dusted her lace dress. I had to admit, it was very pretty. "Coming?" she asked me. She looked like Queen Alexa again.

I stood up too. "Sure." I followed her to the patio doors.

We were almost outside when I said, "Hey, Alexa? Want to come to my birthday party tomorrow? It won't be a big deal or anything, just pizza and movie night . . ."

She turned around and squealed so loud I jumped. "That would be great!" Then she waggled a finger in my face. "But as the guest of honor, I get to choose the movie!"

12

WORD OF THE DAY

PHENOMENAL

Highly

extraordinary and

impressive

It was raining on Sunday morning. I woke up and thought, *Great! A perfect end to a yucky week.* Instead of the henna party of my dreams, I'd get the exact opposite today.

An un-party.

Then I remembered everything that had happened at Alexa's party. Oh yeah. My life wasn't so bad. I was having a boring old pizza-and-movie birthday, but at least my family would be with me. And my best friend.

Then I remembered something else: Alexa.

I did a little prayer that Alexa would forget all about my invitation yesterday. I hadn't really meant to invite her, obviously.

I had nobody to blame but me. Mama had told me to think before doing something, but I hadn't listened. Again.

I got up from my bed with a groan. I didn't want to think about Alexa coming to my un-party anymore. I bent over and took something from under my bed. It was a bag from Kids Korner, the shop Baba had taken me to yesterday.

I peeked into Aliyah's room. She was lying on her bed, looking at her phone. "What do you want?" she asked, giving me a scowl.

I held the bag out in front me like a shield. "This is for you."

She took the bag and opened it. There was a small glass bottle inside, like the one I'd broken the other day. "They didn't have jasmine, so I got rose instead," I said, trying to be helpful. "Because you like the smell of roses."

She was quiet. Too quiet. She was staring at the bottle like it had a poop emoji on it.

Which it didn't. All it had was a picture of a rose.

I turned to go. "Anyway, sorry I broke your bottle. I won't come into your room again." Well, that last part wasn't exactly a promise. I'd probably need to sneak inside again at some point. But the first part, about being sorry, was very true.

Aliyah finally looked at me. "Thanks, sis."

At breakfast, Baba gave me a whole set of Ramona books. "Told you I had an awesome present for you," he said, smiling.

He was right. Ramona was the awesomest.

The kitchen still reminded me of the burnt casserole, so I went back to my room after breakfast to read my new books.

Hanna arrived at six o'clock, holding a bunch of balloons and a small wrapped gift. "Happy birthday!" she said, smiling very big.

I grinned back. Balloons always cheered me up.

I led her upstairs to my room. "Where's everyone?" she asked. "It's awfully quiet in your house today."

I shrugged. "Who knows?" After the circus of the last few days, I was glad things were quiet again. I closed my door and jumped on the bed. "Okay, let me see my present."

She handed over the box. It was a pair of kitty-ear headphones, just like I'd wanted.

"I love them!" I cried, hugging her. I felt okay now about my un-party. I had my bestie with me, and pretty soon we'd be eating gooey cheese pizza from Marco's. That was the best pizza place in the whole town.

Hanna hugged me back. "That's what best friends are for."

The doorbell rang downstairs. "Is the pizza here already?" Hanna asked.

My stomach jumped. "Oh, I forgot to tell you. We're going to have an extra guest today."

She leapt from the bed and ran downstairs. I followed more slowly. This was going to be terrible. My best friend and my worst enemy were going to be spending pizza-and-movie night together. In my house.

Ugh.

When we got downstairs, Alexa stood with Mama in my living room looking . . . nervous? "Happy birthday," she said awkwardly.

"Thanks," I said in the exact same tone.

Mama pushed us all toward the backyard. "How about we go outside?" she said, smiling.

I frowned. "But it's almost dark now."

Mama didn't stop pushing us. She had this excited look on her face that was very strange. "Just for a bit. Come on!"

I almost stomped my foot, because nobody did what I said even on my birthday. But Hanna and Alexa were already outside, so I followed them. And then stopped. My mouth dropped open.

Mama spread her arms wide. "Ta-da!"

The backyard didn't look anything like our normal backyard. There were fairy lights on the trees, and the big red carpet from our guest room was spread on the grass. Music streamed from big speakers on the patio. Baba and Sal were dressed like waiters, bringing trays of juice and water to us.

"What . . . what?" I spluttered, feeling weak.

Alexa and Hanna sighed. "Wow, this is so pretty!" they cried together.

There were right. It was phenomenal! And very familiar. I turned to see Aliyah smiling at me. "Just like your sketch, isn't it?" she asked.

It was exactly like my sketch. I noticed Aliyah waving a henna cone around. Under her arm, she held her yellow design book. "Welcome to the Khan Henna Party!" she said. "Who wants to go first?"

I think I squealed. I can't be sure. And then I got to go first, because I was the birthday girl. I choose a peacock design, with flowers all around, like a garden.

Hanna chose a star pattern, and Alexa chose a bunch of vines that looked very cool. The three of us sat on patio chairs while the henna dried. Mostly we talked about school, how Miss Piccolo was totally mean for giving us a surprise quiz on Friday, and how the playground needed a new swing set. Then Hanna told us all about Mr. Trenton's magical journey act. Alexa and I had totally missed it while we sat behind her living room couch feeling sorry for ourselves.

I looked at Alexa's face. Was she still sad about her parents missing her party? She was admiring her henna with a big smile, so I guess she was happy. She looked nothing like Queen Alexa right now.

"Marya!" Dadi called to me from the patio.

I got up and went over to hug her. "Isn't this nice?" I whispered.

"Just like my show," she agreed. Then she turned me around and put something around my neck. "Happy birthday!"

I looked down. It was the necklace I'd found under Dadi's bed. "This is for me?"

She gave me a little pat on my cheek. "Of course. I was hiding it under my bed. Why do you think I was mad you found it?"

I hugged her again and went back to my friends. Well, one friend and one . . . Alexa.

"I thought Operation Help the Khans was a failure," Hanna said. "How did your parents agree to all this?"

Mama heard her. "Marya had some accidents,

but her heart was in the right place," she said. "And this was all Aliyah's idea."

I blinked and stared at my big sister. "Really?" I whispered.

Aliyah rolled her eyes at me. "That still doesn't mean you can come in my room."

I grinned. This henna party was just . . . perfect.

Only then, the doorbell rang and Marco's pizza was delivered, and the party became even more perfect.

Now it's your turn! Color in the henna design or trace it on a piece of paper and transfer onto your palms.

ABOUT THE AUTHOR
AND ILLUSTRATOR

Saadia Faruqi was born in Pakistan and moved to the United States when she was twenty-two years old. She writes the Yasmin series and popular middle-grade novels such as *Yusuf Azeem Is Not a Hero*. Besides writing books for kids, she also loves reading, binge-watching her favorite shows, and taking naps. She lives in Houston with her family.

Ani Bushry graduated from the University of West England with a background in graphic design and illustration. She grew up listening to stories her mom told her and always wanted to tell her own. She lives in the Maldives with her husband and cat, Lilo, whom she loves to spoil.